Katie Woo

Katie Woo, Super Scout

by Fran Manushkin

illustrated by Tammie Lyon

PICTURE WINDOW BOOKS
a capstone imprint

Katie Woo is published by Picture Window Books,
A Capstone Imprint
1710 Roe Crest Drive
North Mankato, Minnesota 56003
www.capstonepub.com

Text © 2016 Fran Manushkin
Illustrations © 2016 Picture Window Books

Library of Congress Cataloging-in-Publication Data
Manushkin, Fran, author.
  Katie Woo, super scout / by Fran Manushkin; illustrated by Tammie Lyon.
     pages cm. — (Katie Woo)
Summary: On a hike with the Super Scouts, Katie is paired up with a girl she does not know who seems much better at scouting then Katie is, but eventually Katie finds that she has discovered a new friend.
ISBN 978-1-4795-6178-0 (hardcover) — ISBN 978-1-4795-6180-3 (pbk.) — ISBN 978-1-4795-6189-6 (ebook pdf)
1. Woo, Katie (Fictitious character)—Juvenile fiction. 2. Chinese Americans—Juvenile fiction. 3. Scouts (Youth organization members)—Juvenile fiction. 4. Hiking—Juvenile fiction. 5. Friendship—Juvenile fiction. [1. Chinese Americans—Fiction. 2. Scouting (Youth activity)—Fiction. 3. Hiking—Fiction. 4. Friendship—Fiction.] I. Lyon, Tammie, illustrator. II. Title. III. Series: Manushkin, Fran. Katie Woo.
  PZ7.M3195Kbk 2015
  813.54—dc23
[E]   2014041798

Art Director: Kay Fraser
Graphic Designer: Kristi Carlson

Photo Credits:
Greg Holch, pg. 26
Tammie Lyon, pg. 26
Vector images, Shutterstock ©

Printed in the United States of America in North Mankato, Minnesota
042019   000076

Table of Contents

Chapter 1
Scout Sisters

Katie and JoJo joined the

Super Scouts.

JoJo read the Scout Pledge:

"We promise to treat all

scouts like sisters."

"That's cool!" said Katie.

"I've always wanted sisters."

Their leader, Miss Harris,

said, "Today, we are going

for a hike in the woods.

Please pick a partner."

Janie, a girl Katie didn't know, asked, "Will you be my partner?"

"Sure!" said Katie. "Hello, sister!"

"Our hike is a treasure hunt," said Miss Harris.

"Yay!" yelled Katie. "I'm great at those."

"I'm not," said Janie.

"Don't worry!" said Katie. "I'll help you."

Janie read. "We need to find three things. The first one is a bug that fits on a penny."

"Ew, bugs!" said Katie.

"Yay, bugs!" cheered Janie.

As they walked, Janie
called, "Come here, bugs,
bugs, bugs."

Katie yelled, "Go *away*,
bugs, bugs, bugs!"

Janie picked up a beetle

and put it on a penny. "Isn't

he cute?" she asked.

"Yech!" said

Katie. "Not

to me."

"Yay!" said Janie. "The

bug is our first treasure."

Chapter 2

Fairy Calling

"Now we need to find

the second treasure," said

Katie. "It's something blue.

That sounds easy. I'm sure

I'll find it first."

But Katie didn't. Janie did.

"I found it!" she yelled. "It's

these pretty blue periwinkles."

Katie felt bad. She said,

"Why can't I find any

treasures?"

Katie made a mean face

at Janie and said, "I should

have gone with JoJo. We

always have fun."

Janie looked sad, but she

didn't say anything.

Janie went off by herself.

After a while, she began

grabbing twigs and stacking

them up.

"What are you doing?"

asked Katie.

"I'm making

a fairy house,"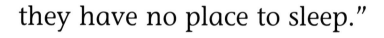

said Janie.

"They live in

the forest, but

the forest, but

they have no place to sleep."

"What a nice thing to

do!" said Katie. "Can I help

you?"

"Sure!" agreed Janie.

Katie made a leafy roof,

and Janie lined the path to

the house with acorns.

"Here, fairies!" they called.

"I think fairies come at night," said Janie.

"Me too," agreed Katie. "It was fun making the house with you."

"I'm glad," said Janie. "Now let's find the last treasure."

Chapter 3
Treasure and Treats

Katie read, "The last treasure must be as yellow as the sun."

"I see it!" Katie pointed. "A pretty birch leaf!"

"Good going!" yelled Janie. "We did it!"

"Hey," Katie said, sniffing the air. "I smell something sweet! Do you?"

"It's s'mores!" they yelled together.

"Let's hurry!" said Katie. "We don't want to miss any!"

Katie and Janie held hands and followed the sweet scent to the campfire — and the other Super Scouts.

Katie told Janie, "I'm sorry I acted stinky. Will you still be my sister?"

"For sure!" Janie smiled. "Sometimes sisters might fight. But they are still sisters."

"Sisters, sisters, hurray!" chanted Katie.

The Super Scouts gathered around the campfire. Katie said, "Janie, come sit with me and JoJo."

JoJo made room for her.

"Let's have some more s'mores," yelled JoJo.

"Yes!" said Katie. "You can't have too many s'mores or sisters."

And it was true!

About the Author

Fran Manushkin is the author of many popular picture books, including *Baby, Come Out!*; *Latkes and Applesauce: A Hanukkah Story*; *The Tushy Book*; *The Belly Book*; and *Big Girl Panties*. There is a real Katie Woo — she's Fran's great-niece — but she never gets in half the trouble of the Katie Woo in the books. Fran writes on her beloved Mac computer in New York City, without the help of her two naughty cats, Chaim and Goldy.

About the Illustrator

Tammie Lyon began her love for drawing at a young age while sitting at the kitchen table with her dad. She continued her love of art and eventually attended the Columbus College of Art and Design, where she earned a bachelor's degree in fine art. After a brief career as a professional ballet dancer, she decided to devote herself full time to illustration. Today she lives with her husband, Lee, in Cincinnati, Ohio. Her dogs, Gus and Dudley, keep her company as she works in her studio.

Glossary

acorns (AY-korns)—the seeds of an oak tree

fairy (FAIR-ee)—a magical creature such as a tiny person with wings, found in fairy tales

partner (PART-nur)—one of two or more people who do something together

periwinkles (PAIR-ee-wing-kuhls)—evergreen herbs that spread along the ground and have shiny leaves and blue or white flowers

squeezing (SKWEEZ-ing)—pressing firmly together from opposite sides

treasure (TREZH-ur)—gold, jewels, money, or other valuable things that have been collected or hidden

Discussion Questions

1. How do you think Katie felt after Janie found the first two treasures? How do you know?

2. Would you like to be in a scouting group? Why or why not?

3. Janie tells Katie that sometimes sisters fight. Have you ever gotten in a fight with a sibling or friend? What happened and how did you resolve it?

Writing Prompts

1. Pretend that you get to create a treasure hunt of your own. Write a list of three things that hunters need to find.

2. The Super Scouts spend a lot of time outside. Write a paragraph about your favorite thing to do outside.

3. Design and draw a new Super Scout uniform for Katie. Then write a paragraph describing your design and explaining your choices.

Having Fun with Katie Woo!

In the story, Katie and Janie make a fairy house using things they find in the woods. You can make a fairy house of your own while out hiking. Or follow these directions for a fun indoor craft.

Fairy House Fun

What you need:

- an empty 20-oz soda bottle, washed and dried

- styrofoam cup (the opening should be wide enough to securely sit on top of the bottle)

- moss paper

- burlap fabric, cut into small strips

- glue

- yellow paper

- small sticks, leaves, seeds, stones, etc. for decorations

What you do:

1. Wrap and glue the moss paper around the soda bottle to cover the bottom 6-7 inches.

2. To make windows and a door, cut small squares or circles out of the yellow paper. Glue the shapes on the house. Then glue small twigs around the shape to make window and door frames.

3. To make the roof, glue burlap strips over the cup until the cup is covered, making sure that the burlap hangs over the rim slightly. Add leaves, seeds, or sticks to decorate the roof.

4. Place the cup upside down on the top of the bottle. If you would like more decorations, add them. Else your house is ready for fairies!

THE FUN DOESN'T STOP HERE!

Discover more at www.capstonekids.com

💜 Videos & Contests

❀ Games & Puzzles

💜 Friends & Favorites

❀ Authors & Illustrators

Find cool websites and more books like this one at www.facthound.com. Just type in the Book ID: **9781479561780** and you're ready to go!